Dear Parents and Educators,

Welcome to Penguin Young Readers! As parents and educators, you know that each child develops at his or her own pace—in terms of speech, critical thinking, and, of course, reading. Penguin Young Readers recognizes this fact. As a result, each Penguin Young Readers book is assigned a traditional easy-to-read level (1–4) as well as a Guided Reading Level (A–P). Both of these systems will help you choose the right book for your child. Please refer to the back of each book for specific leveling information. Penguin Young Readers features esteemed authors and illustrators, stories about favorite characters, fascinating nonfiction, and more!

Otis's Busy Day

LEVEL 1

GUIDED READING LEVEL **C**

This book is perfect for an **Emergent Reader** who:
• can read in a left-to-right and top-to-bottom progression;
• can recognize some beginning and ending letter sounds;
• can use picture clues to help tell the story; and
• can understand the basic plot and sequence of simple stories.

Here are some **activities** you can do during and after reading this book:
• Character Traits: Even though Otis is a tractor, he can act and feel just like you do. Make a list of traits that describe him.
• Sight Words: Sight words are frequently used words that readers know just by looking at them. These words are not "sounded out" or "decoded"; rather they are known instantly, on sight. Knowing these words helps children develop into efficient readers. The words listed below are sight words used in this book. As you read or reread the story, have the child point out the sight words.

are	he	look
down	is	this
go	it	up
good	jumps	what

Remember, sharing the love of reading with a child is the best gift you can give!

—Bonnie Bader, EdM
Penguin Young Readers program

W9-BON-298

*Penguin Young Readers are leveled by independent reviewers applying the standards developed by Irene Fountas and Gay Su Pinnell in *Matching Books to Readers: Using Leveled Books in Guided Reading*, Heinemann, 1999.

To tractor friends and
new readers everywhere —LL

PENGUIN YOUNG READERS
Published by the Penguin Group
Penguin Group (USA) LLC, 375 Hudson Street, New York, New York 10014, USA

USA | Canada | UK | Ireland | Australia | New Zealand | India | South Africa | China

penguin.com
A Penguin Random House Company

Art copyright © 2009, 2011, 2013 by Loren Long. Text copyright © 2014 by Loren Long.
All rights reserved. Published by Penguin Young Readers, an imprint of Penguin Group (USA) LLC,
345 Hudson Street, New York, New York 10014.
Manufactured in China.

Library of Congress Cataloging-in-Publication Data is available.

ISBN 978-0-448-48130-2 (pbk)   10 9 8 7 6
ISBN 978-0-448-48131-9 (hc)   10 9 8 7 6 5 4 3 2

FROM #1 *NEW YORK TIMES* BESTSELLING LOREN LONG

Otis's Busy Day

by Loren Long

Penguin Young Readers
An Imprint of Penguin Group (USA) LLC

This is Otis.

He is a tractor.

Otis is having a busy day.

He pulls.

He sings.

He dances.

Otis goes up.

Otis goes down.

Otis jumps.

Otis zips.

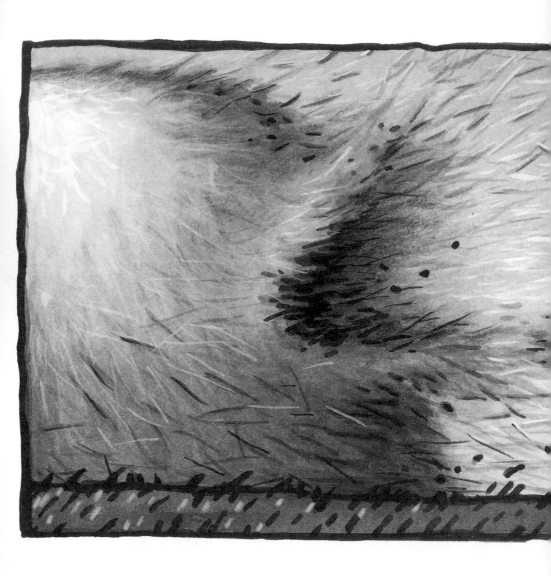

Look, a friend!

Otis gives him a ride.

They are tired.

What a busy day!

It is time to go home.

Good night, Otis.